12/93

W9-BZB-887

THE LEGEND OF
SLAPPY HOOPER

THE LEGEND OF SLAPPY HOOPER

An American Tall Tale

Retold by Aaron Shepard • Pictures by Toni Goffe

CHARLES SCRIBNER'S SONS · NEW YORK
Maxwell Macmillan Canada · Toronto
Maxwell Macmillan International
New York · Oxford · Singapore · Sydney

For Chuck Ellsworth and the Allpoints crew

—A. S.

For Tim and Sue

—T.G.

Text copyright © 1993 by Aaron Shepard
Illustrations copyright © 1993 by Toni Goffe

Charles Scribner's Sons Books for Young Readers
Macmillan Publishing Company • 866 Third Avenue, New York, NY 10022

Maxwell Macmillan Canada, Inc.
1200 Eglinton Avenue East, Suite 200 • Don Mills, Ontario M3C 3N1

Macmillan Publishing Company is part of
the Maxwell Communication Group of Companies.

First edition   10 9 8 7 6 5 4 3 2 1
Printed in Singapore

Library of Congress Cataloging-in-Publication Data
Shepard, Aaron.
    The legend of Slappy Hooper : an American tall tale / adapted by
Aaron Shepard ; pictures by Toni Goffe. — 1st ed.
        p.   cm.
    Summary: Slappy Hooper, the world's biggest, fastest, bestest sign
painter, gets in all kinds of trouble with his amazingly realistic signs.
    ISBN 0-684-19535-6
    [1. Folklore—United States. 2. Tall tales.]   I. Goffe, Toni, ill. II. Title.
PZ8.1.S53945Le 1993   398.21—dc20   [E]   92-18153

A similar version of *The Legend of Slappy Hooper* was published
in *Cricket* magazine in 1990.

You've heard about Paul Bunyan, the greatest lumberjack of all time. And you've heard about Pecos Bill, the greatest cowboy. Now let me tell you about Slappy Hooper, the world's biggest, fastest, bestest sign painter.

You'd better believe Slappy was biggest! Why, he was seven feet tall with shoulders to match, and he weighed three hundred pounds, even without his cap and coverall and brush and bucket.

And fastest? Just give him an eight-inch brush. *Slip! slop! slap!* The job was done—and so smooth, you'd never see a brushstroke.

And you bet Slappy was bestest! That was on account of his pictures. No one else ever made them so true to life.

In fact, some folks said they were *too* true to life.

Slappy's trouble started with the huge red rose he painted on the sign for Rose's Florist Shop.

"Slappy, it's so real!" said Miss Rose Red, the owner. "Why, I can just about smell the fragrance!"

But a week later, Rose Red fluttered into Slappy's sign shop. "Slappy, that sign of yours was *too good*. The bees got wind of it and swarmed all over that rose, trying to get in. They scared away all my customers! That was bad enough, but wait till you see what's happened now!"

When they reached the florist shop, Slappy saw that the bees were gone. But the rose had withered and died.

"No one buys from a florist with a withered flower on her sign," said Rose Red. "That's the last thing you'll paint for *me,* Slappy Hooper!"

The story got around, but most folks just laughed, and they still wanted Slappy to do their signs. His next job was to paint a billboard for the Eagle Messenger Service. Slappy painted an eagle three times larger than life.

"Amazing!" said Mr. Baldwin Eagle. "It's so real, I could swear I saw it blink! Wait a minute. I *did* see it blink!"

Then the bird flapped its wings and flew right off the billboard.

"That sign was *too good,*" said Mr. Eagle. "That's the last time you'll work for *me,* Slappy Hooper!"

Folks were getting scared to hire Slappy. But at last he got a job from the Sunshine Travel Agency. The billboard was to show a man and woman on a beach, toasting under a hot sun. Slappy painted it the day after a big snowstorm.

"Wonderful!" said Mr. Ray Sunshine. "Why, that sun makes me feel hot. And look! The snow on the sidewalk is melting!"

But a couple of days later, Slappy got a call.

"Slappy, your sign is *too good*. Get down here right away!"

When Slappy arrived, he saw that the sidewalk and street in front of the billboard were covered with beach chairs. People sat around in swimsuits and sunglasses, sipping lemonade and splashing suntan lotion.

"They're blocking traffic, and the mayor blames me!" said Mr. Sunshine. "Besides, they won't need my travel agency if they take their vacations here! You've got to do something, Slappy."

So Slappy set up his gear and got to work. He painted the sun on the billboard much hotter. Before long, the crowd was sweating buckets and complaining of sunburn. Then everyone packed up and left.

"Good work, Slappy," said Mr. Sunshine. Then he gasped. "Look at that!"

The man and woman on the billboard were walking off, too.

Just then, a lick of flame shot up the wall of the building across the street. Slappy's sign had set it on fire! In a few minutes, fire trucks clanged up and firefighters turned hoses on the flames.

"Slappy!" said Mr. Sunshine. "Try something else!"

Slappy got back to work. He painted a storm cloud across that sun. But he had to jump clear when the cloud shot bolts of lightning!

Then the storm broke. Slappy's cloud rained so hard, the billboard overflowed and flooded all of Main Street.

Mr. Sunshine cried, "*Never again,* Slappy Hooper!"

After that, no one on earth would hire Slappy. It looked as if his sign-painting days were done.

Slappy felt so low, he made up his mind to throw his paint kit in the river. He dragged it onto the tallest bridge in town and was just about to chuck it, when a voice thundered out beside him.

"Don't dump that gear, Slappy. You're going to need it!"

Right next to Slappy stood a man almost as big as Slappy himself. He wore a paint-splotched white coverall and a cap with two little angel wings sticking out. He carried an eight-inch brush.

"Who are *you*?" said Slappy.

"I'm Michael, from the Heavenly Sign Company," thundered the man. "The Boss has had an eye on you for some time, Slappy, and He likes your work. He's got a job for you—if you don't mind working in the rain."

"Tell me about it," said Slappy.

"We need someone to paint a rainbow this Wednesday," said Michael. "Most of the time, we handle all the rainbows ourselves. But it's going to rain in a bunch of places Wednesday, and we could sure use some help."

"I'm your man," said Slappy.

That Wednesday morning, Slappy rented a cannon and set it in a big cow pasture. He tied two ropes to his scaffold, then ran the other ends through a couple of skyhooks. Then he loaded the skyhooks in the cannon and shot them straight up.

Sure enough, the skyhooks caught on the sky.

Slappy felt the first raindrops. He piled all his paints and brushes onto his scaffold, climbed on, and hoisted himself up, up, and up!

He kept going till he was just under the clouds. Then he tied his ropes and started to paint.

Slip! slop! slap!

Slappy had only just finished when the sun popped through the clouds and lit up what he'd done.

There never was a finer rainbow! It had every color you could imagine, each one blending perfectly with the next. And not a brushstroke in sight.

Just then, Slappy felt a big jolt. He looked up to see what had caused it.

The sun had run smack into his skyhooks!

Slappy shut his eyes and waited for the long drop to the ground. But it never came. When Slappy looked again, he saw why.

His hooks had caught on the sun itself. And the sun was pulling his rig across the sky!

Now, another sign painter might have been frightened. But not Slappy Hooper. He was enjoying the ride.

He'd covered a good distance when Michael appeared on the scaffold beside him. "The Boss liked your rainbow, Slappy," thundered Michael.

"You mean, it wasn't *too good*?" said Slappy.

"If it isn't *too good,* it's not good enough!" said Michael. "That's how *we* figure. Anyhow, now that you're here, the Boss has another job for you—if you don't mind working odd hours."

"Tell me about it," said Slappy.

"It's the sunrise and sunset," said Michael. "I guess you know, the Boss Himself has been painting them since time began. But He's done it so long, He'd like to give someone else a chance."

"I'm your man," said Slappy Hooper.

Slappy's been up there ever since. Of course, you can't see him, with the sun so bright—but he's there all the same.

Night and day, the sun pulls Slappy and his rig around the world. And every time Slappy comes to a horizon, he reaches up with his eight-inch brush.

Slip! slop! slap! The job is done.

And never a brushstroke in sight.

The legend of "Slappy Hooper, World's Biggest, Fastest, and Bestest Sign Painter" was collected in Chicago in 1938 by Jack Conroy for the Federal Writers' Project of the Works Progress Administration. It was first published in B. A. Botkin's *A Treasury of American Folklore* (Crown, New York, 1944).

Carl Sandburg, in the foreword to Botkin's book, called the legend "a fresh modern masterpiece that will not fail to be passed along from generation to generation."

Legends are built piece by piece, by many hands. Conroy himself presented only a selection of Slappy's exploits. So, in the storyteller tradition, I've included new adventures of the world's greatest sign painter.

—A.S.